Carol's Christmas

ROMANCING THE SPIRIT SERIES

CB SAMET

Carol's Christmas

CB SAMET

"Heartwarming stand alone novellas, each with their own supernatural twist. From Egypt to a small town, old love rekindled to new loves and loves that last the centuries. Each book perfect to cuddle up with on a chilly day and escape into romance that never dies."

AUTHOR H.M. GOODEN (ON ROMANCING THE SPIRIT SERIES, BOOKS 1-6)

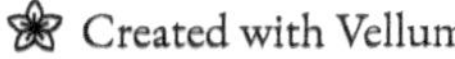 Created with Vellum

One

"She's going to die." Tony Olsen paced the small office in the back of the pawnshop.

"Relax. Everybody dies, Tony." Burke took a drag off the cigarette that perpetually hung from his bottom lip. "I mean, look at the pair of us—a couple of nobody ghosts who don't want to move on."

Tony ran a hand through his gray hair. "But I've seen her death, Burke. Christmas morning. Bam!" He smacked his hands together. "Hit by a delivery truck. A truck!"

He'd watched the vision of Carol's death in slow motion. She walked toward the curb, distracted and not checking traffic. She stepped off into the road, and the truck that hit her didn't have time to slow down, or even swerve.

"There's a lot of tragedy in this world, Tony. She's lived to be forty-two—that's a lot more than some people get."

Burke leaned back in his chair. The chair didn't move or squeak beneath his weight, and there was no noise even as he clumped his feet up onto the office desk.

"Besides," he continued, "from what you've told me about this woman, she don't got much of a life nowadays as it is."

Tony shoved his hands in his slacks—his Giorgio Armani suit pants. They were the very ones he'd been buried in when he'd died, five years earlier. Since his death, he'd been lingering as a spirit on earth, watching Carol Sullivan live the same life he'd had—making the same heartless, callous mistakes.

"Well, I'm partly to blame." Tony had never been kind to Carol. As a result of that—and other contributing factors from her past—she'd grown to become as cold and lonely as an iceberg, and drifting into an ever-melting, lifeless existence just the same.

"She can't even hear or see me," Tony continued. "How am I supposed to save her?"

Some living people had a gift—the ability to see and hear ghosts. The so-called mediums, however, were few and far between—and Carol wasn't one of them.

"She doesn't have any friends or family who can see ghosts. Without an intermediary, I can't reach out to her." Tony had been reduced to helplessly watching Carol ruin her life.

Burke pulled the cigarette out of his mouth and flicked nonexistent ashes off the glowing, orange tip. He stared at one walls of the pawnshop—where yellow paint was peeling from the plaster. Tony kept quiet. He recognized Burke's narrow-eyed gaze of contemplation.

Tony hadn't known Burke in life. He'd never have associated with a pawnshop owner. In death however, Burke had become his best friend. Tony wished he'd taken time to make friendships like this while he'd still been alive—but being a ghost was all about languishing in regret, wasn't it?

Burke scratched at his large belly.

"Save her, eh? Might be a way to—but not in the way you think."

"I'll try anything." Tony couldn't stomach the thought of a talented young surgeon like Carol dying before she recognized the opportunity to turn her life around.

"You can make your case to the Christmas Spirits."

"The Christmas Spirits? They really exist?"

"Of course. Some spirits can be seen by whomever they choose at certain times of the year. The Christmas trio is already *real* busy this time of year, though. They're probably booked up. Some people start booking them a year in advance."

"They could help me help Carol?"

"They don't save lives. They save souls."

Tony's posture slumped. He wanted both for Carol—her life and her soul—and Christmas was only a week away. What were the chances his Christmas miracle could be worked into the busy schedules of the Christmas Spirits?

But he had to try—for Carol.

"So, is it like in the stories?" Tony asked. "The Christmas Spirits can save a soul in one night?" He sighed as he considered this. "They'd have to. She wouldn't have very long to live after that." He pressed the palms of his hands into his eyes, trying to block out the future image he'd seen of Carol getting hit by a truck on Christmas morning.

In his vision, she'd distractedly walked to the curb.

She'd stepped over the edge.

The end.

Burke shrugged, though his eyes looked at Tony with compassion.

"At least she'd have salvation. She can set things in motion to give her peace as a spirit. She wouldn't be lingering, like you—stuck wondering how to fix the cold-hearted deeds of her life."

"Okay. I'll do it. Where can I find the Christmas Spirits?"

"This close to Christmas? They oughta be at Michigan Avenue, under the Chicago Christmas tree."

Two

Carol Sullivan carried a coffee in one hand and her phone in the other as she walked to the surgical intensive care unit. Her heels clicked on the linoleum floor, and her white coat gleamed beneath the fluorescent lights.

On her phone, she checked her email and her schedule. She had an OR case at 10 a.m. and maybe an hour break before two more surgeries. When Carol reached the work station, her physician assistant, John Baker, stood abruptly from where he'd been sitting.

He banged his knee against the countertop in his haste, and rubbed it as he stammered: "Good morning, Dr. Sullivan."

Carol Sullivan appraised Johnny's white coat—which was actually stained a dingy yellow and had frayed elbows. His shoes were the same scuffed, worn Burkenstocks she'd been staring at for years. She'd repeatedly told him to buy new apparel—so he could appear more professional—but he'd ignored her request each and every time.

"What's the status?" Carol snapped.

Johnny handed her a single sheet of paper containing her patient list. "Mr. Smith is recovering nicely. We'll be pulling his chest tube today." Johnny glanced up at her briefly. "The patient was wondering if you'd stop by to see him today. He's day three post-op, and he said he hasn't seen you since his surgery."

Carol blinked irritably. "Johnny, do you know how much insurance pays for an inpatient post-op follow-up visit by a surgeon? Zero. Nada. Nothing. Zilch. That's why I have you. I do the surgeries; you see the patients while they're in the hospital. I get paid for one outpatient clinic follow-up visit—that's it."

Disappointment seemed to ooze from the visible pores on Johnny's broad forehead and generously sized nose.

"I don't make the rules," Carol added with a shrug.

Johnny pushed his glasses up on his nose and continued: "Mr. Johnson's family is asking what the next steps are. He's post-op day twenty-six. He's the one with..."

"...post-op pneumonia. Yes, I know. The plan is; he *can't* recover from his pneumonia—his lungs aren't strong enough. I warned him and his family that resecting his lung cancer was high risk."

"Oh, they understand that. They're not upset about his

care—but they think he wouldn't want to be on life support the way he is now."

Carol's left eye twitched. "They want to pull life support?"

"Yes. If he's not going to survive, they want to stop it."

"Well, they can't. Not until he's post-op day thirty-one. Five days."

"But…"

"Stop gaping at me. You know how damaging thirty-day post-op mortality is to a surgeon and the hospital. Half the thoracic surgeons in the country would've turned down Mr. Johnson's case, but I chose to try to help him. My reward is to have his death increase my thirty-day mortality statistics? I don't think so. Again, I didn't make this rule, and all it does is damage those of us who are willing to be more aggressive. Other surgeons cherry-pick the healthiest cases."

Johnny hesitated. "But he's a patient, not a number."

"If only the national benchmarks we're judged by took that into account," Carol snapped back.

"What do you want me to tell the patient?"

"It's Christmas Eve. They don't want him to die on Christmas. Keep him alive until after Christmas and everyone's had a chance to enjoy the holidays."

Johnny nodded, but looked unconvinced.

Carol sipped her coffee before prompting the physician assistant. "Next patient?"

"The radiation oncologist wants to start Mr. Brown on radiation therapy, but we need to control his atrial fibrillation first."

"Good. Get him moved out of my ICU."

Johnny blinked at her.

Carol pursed her lips. "He's stage four. I can't fix him. I've taken care of his pleural effusion. Now, the intensivists can fix his atrial fibrillation."

"I know—it's just hard on patients to change teams."

"We've got three patients who are going to be post-op by the end of the day. I need those beds open." As if reading Johnny's expression, Carol admitted: "Yes, there's an assembly line to surgery—and, yes, it's impersonal. However, warm and fuzzy doesn't pay anyone's bills."

"Yes, ma'am."

Carol took a deep breath to rein in her frustration. She felt like she shouldn't have to justify all of her actions to her physician assistant. Johnny knew how things functioned on the surgical service. Were his gushing emotions a direct result of the holiday season? Why did people get so sentimental during the period of a commercialized, staged event like Christmas?

Carol glanced at her watch. "I need to scrub in."

"Oh, and your office assistant called," Johnny added. "She said Mr. Forte is asking when he can schedule his lung volume reduction surgery."

Carol raised her hands in the air—phone in one, coffee in the other—indicating the situation was out of her control. "His insurance company won't approve it. If I do the procedure, I'm strapping him with a hefty bill for an elective procedure."

"His breathing is getting worse."

"Of course it is. His upper lobes are like Swiss cheese from emphysema."

"You could appeal the case."

"Did you know that insured people have more medical debt than the uninsured? That is how bad our medical care has gotten. It's unfathomable. People can't even afford deductibles—*deductibles*." She shook her head and left, stalking off toward the OR.

CAROL FINISHED HER PRE-OPERATIVE DOCUMENTATION. While waiting for the OR to open itself to her cases, she walked back to her office in the surgical services building.

"Carol!"

She stiffened—startled at the chipper voice. Then, with a scowl, she turned around.

"Hello, Mel."

Without invitation, Carol's younger sister wrapped her arms around the surgeon and squeezed. Melanie was always cheerful, and Carol suspected pediatricians were all secretly dosed with antidepressants to maintain this state of perpetual happiness. How else could they be able to be all smiles around snot-nosed children, when their reimbursement rates were no better than those of a family doctor, or even a physician assistant?

Mel beamed a smile. "Did you get my text? Are you coming to our Christmas Eve party?"

Carol gestured at her scrubs. "Surgeries."

Melanie's smile remained undeterred. She wore a red knit cap with short curls protruding from beneath the edges. Her sweater was covered with tiny reindeer, set against a backdrop of green and red stripes.

"You should come by when you're done. Pike and I'll be up late celebrating."

Carol fought not to roll her eyes.

Celebrating? That meant gift-giving, junk food-eating, and excessive drinking—all the commercialized pursuits merchants wanted people to indulge in during the Christmas period. Spend. Spend. Spend. Meanwhile, credit card debt across the country soared.

Melanie shook her head. "All work and no play."

Carol pursed her lips. "The need for surgeries doesn't take a break just because the rest of the country does."

Melanie gave Carol a look of pity, even as she maintained her dimpled smile.

"Except it doesn't always have to be *you* doing the surgery, Carol—*every* holiday, *every* year."

Before Carol could protest, Melanie kissed her sister's cheek and bounded away down the hall, back toward the elevator.

CAROL FINISHED her final surgery for the day—a thoracic aortic aneurysm repair—and returned to the physician locker room. It was only four in the afternoon, but most people had already left early since it was Christmas Eve. Apparently, most other people were like her sister Melanie—and wanted to spend the holidays with their families.

Carol didn't share that same sentimentality. Her life was entirely career oriented. She'd chosen between her career and a relationship—and while she felt she shouldn't have *had* to choose, she hadn't worked relentlessly every day and gotten into one of the best surgical residencies in the country, just to give it all up for a man.

Even if he'd been *the man*—the one for her in a way she knew she'd never have again.

So, why bother after that? Carol hadn't. She hadn't dated since Liam left.

She changed out of her scrubs and back into her skirt suit. When she closed her locker, the lights above flickered.

Odd.

The metal doors of the lockers rattled on their hinges.

Carol backed away from them. Was this an earthquake? Here in Chicago? Except, the rest of the room wasn't shaking; only the lockers shimmied.

She felt her heart race. Was she hallucinating? She *had* drunk three cups of coffee today, on a still-empty stomach.

Suddenly, a man emerged from one end of the room.

Carol gasped. In a hoarse voice, she croaked: "This is the women's locker room!"

"Hello, Carol. You look well."

Carol squinted her eyes. "Tony?"

She blinked. "Tony... You—you can't be here."

Carol knew Tony—or *had* known Tony. They'd worked together. He'd died about five years earlier from a heart attack. Carol had even gone to his funeral.

Well, she'd sent flowers—or, maybe it was a wreath.

It didn't matter. She'd had too many cases. She couldn't have cancelled them all for the funeral of a coworker.

The figure of Carol's long-deceased thoracic surgery partner took a step forward.

"It's me, Carol—I'm here. But only for tonight, just this once." Tony walked closer.

He appeared to Carol just as she remembered him—in his seventies, with a full head of gray hair. However, he looked pale. No, more than pale. More than *deathly* pale.

In fact, he looked downright transparent.

"This isn't possible," Carol stammered, taking a step back from him.

"It *is* possible." Tony raised his hands reassuringly. "When you make your life only about you, *this* is possible." He gestured to his ghostly body—because Carol could now see that her former coworker *was* a ghost. "It's possible to be doomed to a spirit existence—a curse for my selfishness."

Carol shook her head, stepping nervously backwards from his shimmering, translucent figure. "W-what do you mean, selfish? You saved lives, Tony! You performed the most surgeries of any thoracic surgeon in the state."

While Carol could hardly claim to have been close to Dr. Tony Olsen, she wouldn't hesitate to admit that he'd been the best thoracic surgeon she'd ever trained under and worked with.

"Oh, I saved lives—just like you," he nodded. "Sure. I performed surgeries—but that was my *job*; and I performed my job with cold detachment. Those were people I was fixing—not cars."

"You can't get attached, Tony—you taught me that. You told me if you showed even the slightest hint of compassion, the medical system would suck the life out of you."

"I was wrong, Carol—*dead* wrong." Tony shrugged. "Now, I'm just dead."

"What *are* you?" Carol's analytical mind was at work. A ghost? Specter? Wraith? What were the differences between them?

"I'm a spirit who can't move on. Don't become like me, Carol."

Carol's temper suddenly flared white hot. "Since when did you give a damn about *me*?"

"Since I died," Tony admitted. "Since I realized I trained you wrong. I emphasized the surgery, not the patient." He paused and then added, "And you're right to be angry—I was just as rotten to you as I was to my patients. I had you work too many long hours. Liam left you because I worked you too hard—just like my wife left me."

Carol stood there, shaking. She hadn't realized Tony had known about Liam. She stiffened. It wasn't any of Tony's business. She wrapped her arms around her waist.

"I haven't eaten today," the surgeon said to herself. "That's all this is." Medically, she knew prolonged fasting could cause delirium. She needed to eat and hydrate, and then she'd stop seeing visions of her old mentor.

The lockers rattled again, and then the room seemed to close in all around her. Carol shrank back, tightening her arms around herself.

"Change, Carol!" Tony warned. "Don't become a lost spirit." He paused, raising a ghostly finger. "Tonight, you'll be visited by three ghosts."

"What? *No.*" Despite her terror, Carol's cynicism rose to the forefront. "This is ludicrous."

"Three..." Tony began in a booming voice.

"...let me guess," Carol interrupted him. "The first one at 1 a.m.?"

Tony blinked. "Yes. How did you know that?"

Carol pinched the bridge of her nose. "No. Stop it, Tony. Whatever this is, you need to make it stop."

"Three ghosts!" Her deceased coworker warned, his voice growing supernaturally deep.

Suddenly, the lockers loomed closer over Carol, and terror overwhelmed her. She began to hyperventilate. Grated metal surrounded her—smothered her—until Carol closed her eyes and screamed in terror.

And then—nothing happened.

Moments later, when Carol dared to open her eyes again, she found the locker room restored to its usual condition—upright and immobile, with a bench in between each row of lockers.

Three

Carol hurried out of the hospital, intending to go directly home and have a large glass of Scotch. She stomped down the street, hands in the pockets of her thick coat, and scarf flapping behind her in the breeze.

Yet, Carol didn't feel the biting cold. She didn't feel anything.

She plowed past Christmas trees, carolers, and stores decorated in green, red and gold. She felt the joy in none of it. It was all sentimental commercialism designed to get people to overspend money they didn't have.

During residency, Carol had been forced to work the holidays. During surgery fellowship, she was the one without a spouse or children, so she'd always been coerced into covering the holiday schedule. Finally, when Carol had earned the clout to make someone *else* work Christmas, she figured—why bother?

Let the rest of them have their celebration and waste their money.

Carol paused at the corner. She had the choice of several paths home, but she always opted for the same one, which took her past the art gallery. She often stopped there during her lunch breaks, or on her way home.

Carol crossed the street. She'd only been intending to walk past it, but was instead surprised to find The Stardust Gallery still open on Christmas Eve.

She walked inside, and the scent of cinnamon wafted toward her with the warm air.

Carol took a familiar path directly to her favorite painting. It was of three horses—black, white, and brown—running through the frothy surf on a beach. Behind them, the setting sun lit the sky in vibrant orange. Something about the image of the glistening beach, wide ocean, and expansive horizon captured a sense of freedom. The horses were free to run—free from riders, free from the confines of a fence, and free from obligation.

Carol looked down at the signature in the bottom left corner: *L Charron.*

"Do you like it?" A man's voice sounded in her ear.

"I love it." Carol surprised herself with that confession. She turned to look at the man who'd asked her, standing beside her on the gallery floor.

"Liam?" Her eyes widened. "Oh, my gosh! *Liam!*"

Without even thinking about it, Carol reached out and

embraced the artist. In the few seconds the hug lasted, the last conversation they'd had flooded into her mind.

Stiffening, Carol stepped back, regaining her composure and straightening her scarf.

She was angry with herself. She'd had no right to hug Liam. That scare in the locker room must have affected her judgment.

"How are you, Carol?"

Liam grinned. He looked magnificent, wearing a sleekly tailored tuxedo. He was clean-shaven, and his wavy dark hair was brushed neatly back.

Carol stared at him. Had it really been five years? Liam looked every bit as good as the day he'd left her. His voice was the same soothing baritone.

"I'm good." Carol cleared her throat. "Really good."

She turned back to the painting. "Your work has always been breathtaking, Liam."

"Thank you." He chuckled softly. "I'm glad you like it. We're having a silent auction—a fund-raiser for the children's hospital."

Carol shook her head with a smile. Liam always gave so much of his hard work to charity. She remembered the many hours he'd spend painting and picking colors. He agonized over every brushstroke—but in the end, his creations always seemed magical.

"Since you like it so much," Liam added, "it would be remiss of me not to mention that it's for sale."

Carol said nothing.

Most days, she always found time to stop by The Stardust Gallery to see this particular painting. She'd never seen Liam here before, though. He didn't involve himself in direct sale of his own work—except, of course, for fundraisers.

Carol stared at the painting. She'd grown so accustomed to seeing Liam's art, to having this small piece of him so close to where she worked, that the thought someone else might buy it annoyed her. She already considered the painting hers.

"The colors are so vibrant," Carol said, staring at the painting. "The brushstrokes capture the powerful muscles of the horses."

But she couldn't buy it. It was impractical. The colors matched nothing in her home, and she didn't have room for the enormity of it, in any case.

Liam had once told her he sought to create masterpieces that people would design a room around, rather than vice versa.

This was such a painting. A masterpiece.

"Did you ever start riding again?" Liam asked.

Still staring at the painting, Carol answered: "No."

She hadn't ridden horses since medical school. It had been a brief passion and a hobby of hers once, made possible by a friend who had let her ride his horses at no cost to her. But the eighty-hour work weeks during residency left no room for passions or hobbies.

Carol stood there stiffly. Although she was so close to Liam, standing with their shoulders nearly touching, she still felt like a great canyon divided them; a gorge filled with memories, regrets, and heartache.

She glanced down at his left hand. There was no ring, but that didn't mean he was single. Even if he was, it certainly did nothing to bridge the gaping divide between them.

A stocky, balding man came and stood on the other side of her and appraised the painting.

"It's *not* for sale," Carol snapped.

The man turned and looked up at her, eyes wide. Then, nervously, he moved to the next painting.

"Are you intending on buying it?" Liam asked with an amused tone.

"No." She paused. "I don't know. *He* can't have it."

Liam shook his head, expressing the disappointment she knew all too well. He stuck his hands into his pant pockets.

"Same old Carol. You can't bring yourself to indulge in the beauty and enjoyment of life."

Carol opened her mouth to criticize Liam, but his soft, sad eyes stole the fight from her. Instead, she felt the corners of her lips curl.

"Same old Liam—always trying to revive love in the world, one masterpiece at a time."

He gave her a smile that had Carol instantly wanting to crawl back into his arms.

Instead, she pulled her coat tighter around her and snapped: "I should go." She paused, before adding: "I hope your auction does well."

"It was wonderful to see you again, Carol."

A lump formed in the back of her throat. "Goodbye, Liam."

A moment later, she stumbled back out onto the street —where it was the cold that stung her eyes. She stomped down the sidewalk, arms wrapped around herself.

How could her emotions for Liam still be so strong after five years?

How could he stand there and talk so civilly after everything that had happened?

He left me, she reminded herself.

Carol walked fast toward home, plowing through carolers and avoiding eye contact with all the people peddling for donations.

She wasn't hungry, but she stopped and ordered dumplings and egg-drop soup from a Chinese takeout restaurant one block from her brownstone anyway.

Once she finally arrived home, Carol traded her skirt for cotton pajama bottoms and ate in the quiet stillness of her home in front of her computer.

While she ate, she reviewed labs and chest x-rays through the electronic healthcare record system. Then, she tossed her trash, and moved from her couch to her bed, where she reviewed a few medical journals in her field followed by a final breeze through her email.

When Carol couldn't keep her eyes open any longer, she drifted into a deep sleep.

CAROL WOKE to the darkness of her bedroom and a scratching noise against one widow.

She turned her head and focused her eyes—and saw a clawed, gnarled hand scraping along the outside of her window.

Carol was instantly awake. She bolted upright and blinked in terror, but it wasn't a hand scraping the window

—it was just a bare, black branch with the moonlit sky serving as backdrop. The wind had caused the tentacle-like twigs of the branch to scrape against her window.

Heart still pounding, Carol reached for her phone as she tossed the blanket off.

1 a.m.

A shuffling noise suddenly emerged from her living room, and Carol's heart started pounding again. She sucked in a breath, quietly slipping out of bed and pulling her robe around her.

The shuffling noise continued. This wasn't her imagination—someone was out there!

Should she turn the light on? Wouldn't that make her as visible to her attacker as her attacker would be to her?

Carol looked around desperately for a weapon, but found only a shoe. She picked it up anyway, brandishing it like a weapon with the point of the heel facing out.

With the shoe extended in her trembling hand, Carol tiptoed out of her bedroom, down the hallway, and into the living room.

By the light of a gentle moon, she saw no dangerous figures standing in the darkness.

Heart still pounding, she scanned the shadows—but nothing threatening emerged.

Damn, Tony.

He'd gotten her worked up for nothing.

Distant music suddenly sounded. Carol turned, watching as the edges of her front door became framed in bright, white light.

Was this a prank?

She trod closer to the door, trying to listen over the

sound of her pounding heart. What was that music? *Silent Night*?

Was it carolers? Out this late?

Carol wrenched the front door open, ready to angrily scold whoever was waking her up in the middle of the nigh, only to find a small child standing on her doorstep—a child of perhaps seven or eight.

The chorus of singing dwindled to a stop. Carol stood there and looked down. A glowing halo of light was surrounding the curly, red hair of the little girl on Carol's doorstep.

The little girl looked angelic, and had Carol gaping in awe...

...until stark terror suddenly struck her.

Three ghosts!

She wrenched her silk robe tighter around her, and in a breathless whisper demanded: "Are you the first?"

The little girl nodded softly. "I'm the Ghost of Christmas Past." Her voice was gentle and high-pitched.

Carol sucked in a breath.

"Well, what if I don't want to see the past?"

"Surely, you wouldn't close the door to your own chance at redemption, would you?"

"Redemption," Carol scoffed. "I help people every day. You're telling me that's not enough?"

"You do your job, and people are helped because of it—but you do what benefits you and your financial status. Your job is noble, but your tactics are not. Your intentions have become tainted."

Carol narrowed her eyes at the spirit. She might *look* like a child—with her red plaid skirt, black tights, and pine-green sweater—but she didn't *talk* like one.

Carol tied off her robe with a huff. "Okay. Let's get this over with, then."

The Ghost of Christmas Past extended her arm, and Carol dropped the shoe she'd forgotten she'd been holding. She took the small child's hand, pulling the door of her brownstone closed behind her.

Something that felt like a frightening leap of faith engulfed Carol. All around them, the Christmas decorations on the other brownstones started to glow brighter and brighter, before finally blurring into great smears of green, red, and white.

Carol blinked several times, and when her vision cleared, she found herself outside a row of small townhouses. They were decorated with meager strings of Christmas lights and the buildings looked faded and dingy. Small yards were closed in with chain-link fences.

A dark-haired girl was being dropped off by a school bus, and she lugged her backpack over to one of the townhouse doors. After pulling a key from around her neck, she unlocked the door and let herself inside.

The Ghost of Christmas Past followed the little girl, and Carol followed the ghost—in through the front door of her childhood home. This was a place she'd almost forgotten. It looked even more desolate than she'd remembered it.

Inside, all the rooms were tiny. Even the kitchen was so small that nobody could get access the refrigerator if someone else was cooking at the stove.

The walls were covered in peeling, floral wallpaper—

yellowed from time and stains. The smell of stale cigarettes hung in the air.

When the little girl crept quietly to her room, Carol and the ghost followed. Carol recalled how she'd had to be quiet whenever she came home from school, because her mother worked nights and didn't want Carol waking her up.

"You remember this place?" the ghost asked.

"I remember," Carol said flatly. "Mom worked nights. Dad worked days. They didn't see much of each other— or me."

The girl—Young Carol—flopped onto her bed in her tiny bedroom and opened a Nancy Drew book.

"You liked to read books," the ghost said. "You liked fiction."

"I liked escaping every afternoon into a book," Carol retorted. "I could enter a world in which I wasn't an unwanted child, a nuisance, and another mouth to feed."

Perhaps that was harsh. Carol's parents had always kept her and her sister fed, in school, and in a safe environment. They'd provided adequately for them—but Carol couldn't ever remember feeling truly cherished.

She watched her younger self turn the page of her book.

"It was in one of those adventures that I decided to pursue medicine." The ghost looked up at Carol, her red curls swaying from the motion. "*Nancy Drew. Case File number 35, Bad Medicine.*"

Carol chuckled. "That's right."

It was after reading that book that Carol had solidified how she'd wanted to help people—to better society. She'd planned to make a difference and be someone worthy of note—someone worthy of the affection of others.

Someone who was more than just an annoying kid with a key around their neck and an overactive imagination.

Carol did the math in her head. Her sister Melanie would still have been at daycare during the time of this memory. When Melanie was old enough for grade school, she became Carol's responsibility—a parent when they had no parents present. Carol had cooked for her and her sister and made sure Melanie did her homework.

When Carol had turned thirteen, her parents, who'd already lived practically separate lives beneath the same roof, finally divorced.

Despite her parent's unconcealed disinterest in each other, the separation had still been a shock to young Carol. Melanie, five years younger, had taken it hard as well, and Carol had felt she'd have to put on a front of toughness for Melanie's sake.

Carol had spent her teen years only seeing her father on occasional weekends and holidays—all of which she'd had to arrange herself, since her parents only spoke to each other through their respective lawyers.

After Carol had finally left for college, many years after this memory had taken place, she hadn't bothered coming back home except to see Melanie.

"What happened to that child? The one who dreamed of making the world a better place?" The ghost blinked up at Carol.

"Reality," Carol replied, coldly.

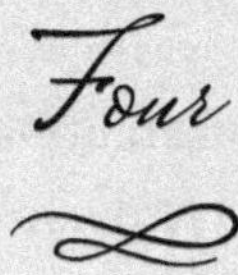

Four

The house aged before Carol's eyes—the wallpaper peeling further and becoming a dingier yellow while the furniture shifted and changed as it was replaced over the years. She then found herself watching a twenty-year-old version of herself sneak into the house, carrying two glasses of eggnog and a gold, foil-wrapped present under her arm.

With the stealth of a mouse, twenty-year-old-Carol had slipped into Melanie's room.

Carol had been away at college at the time of this memory; but remembered returning on this occasion to spend the holiday with her family—or rather Melanie, since their mother was working.

"Carol!"

"Shhh. Merry Christmas." Carol handed Melanie a glass of eggnog and the wrapped gift. "It's after midnight, so I thought we'd celebrate together now."

"Why didn't you give this to me earlier tonight? When we did family gift exchange?" Melanie hugged her sister. "Besides, you already gave me a gift."

Young Carol took a sip of eggnog as she sat beside Melanie on the on the bed.

"Those were cheap decoy earrings," she explained. "This is the *real* gift. I can't give it to you in front of Mom. You know how she gets all huffy when we spend too much money on frivolous things."

"Oh? Something frivolous?" Melanie held the box next to hear ear and shook it with eager anticipation. Then, she dropped it into her lap before tearing off the paper with the ferocity of a groundhog clawing through dirt.

When she opened the gift, Melanie gasped. "It's the dress!"

She leapt out of bed and held the gown against her body. "Mom said I couldn't have it!"

"Well, Mom didn't buy it."

"But it was expensive!"

"Shhh." Carol shrugged. "I've been tutoring organic chemistry. Besides, you look gorgeous in it, and I know you want to go to prom."

Present-day Carol hugged herself as she watched the memory replay in front of her. "She did look beautiful that night."

"You doted on her like your mother never doted on you," the ghost responded.

"I sure did." Carol's sighed. "Probably spoiled her rotten."

Except Carol knew Melanie was anything but rotten, and she'd gone on to become a pediatrician adored by both children and their parents. Carol was so proud of her.

But Melanie gave too much of herself. People took advantage—both of her time, and her money. Melanie would never retire the way she earned so little and spent so much—mostly on other people. Her sister's husband—a graphic designer—wasn't any more frugal than Melanie, but his heart was just as big and sappy as hers.

THEN, the room twisted and contorted around them again, until it finally morphed into a completely different location. This was an office—the walls decorated with numerous bookshelves, all stuffed with medical textbooks. Diplomas and plaques hung from the walls.

This was no Christmas memory.

Carol saw herself at the age of twenty-four—with her long hair flowing down her back. She was sitting in the office across from a stony-faced man behind a desk.

Carol's stomach clenched. She remembered this man— this surgeon—all too well. He'd been in charge of the medical student surgical rotation, and he'd had the cruelest reputation for pimping students and belittling them on rounds. Surviving his wrath had been like surviving a hazing.

"Dr. Sullivan," the stony-faced man began, looking down at twenty-four-year-old Carol over his long, curved nose, "you don't want to be a surgeon."

"I do, sir," Carol replied. "I'm here to ask you for a letter of recommendation for my ERAS, because that's exactly what I want to be."

Carol was applying for residency, and she needed a letter from a surgeon endorsing her qualifications for a surgical specialty.

"Women sometimes *think* they want to specialize in surgery," the doctor's tone was cooly patronizing, "but they truly don't."

"They don't?"

"A four-week surgical rotation in medical school doesn't open your eyes to the demands of a surgeon. There are no work hour restrictions in the *real* world. Women pick surgery—and then they'll either change courses, or back out completely when they decide it's too difficult or they want a family."

A family? What business was it of this man if Carol wanted a family? She didn't even know if *she* wanted one. How could *he* know?

But the man continued: "It's a waste to fill a surgical residency spot with a woman who won't have the commitment to complete it, or the fortitude to become a dedicated surgeon."

Carol watched the eyes of her younger self grow wider, and her cheeks flush. She recalled being absolutely speechless at this humiliating encounter—a clear demonstration of sexual discrimination.

This man had known nothing of Carol's fortitude or dedication, but he had decided neither were sufficient based on her gender alone.

Present-day Carol paced the room and crossed her arms as the past version of herself sat in silent shock.

"Arrogant prick," Carol hissed. *"Save the spots for the men. They're better for the job."* She sneered angrily: "How many women did this monster turn away from surgical residencies with this speech?"

The old surgeon folded his hands on his desk. "Why don't you take some time to think it over? You could consider pediatrics—or, with your excellent grades, you could go to a dermatology residency."

"I wished I'd had the courage to give that jerk a piece of my mind," Carol said, watching her twenty-four-year-old-self squirm in the chair.

"But you didn't," the Ghost of Christmas Past reminded her, "and he did write you that letter."

"Damn right he did." Carol blew out a huff of air.

"You showed him," the little red-headed ghost added.

"Yes, I did."

"You became the dedicated, ruthless surgeon working long hours and forsaking a family that he didn't think you capable of."

Carol shot the ghost a sharp look. Before she could reply, the stuffy office—three-sizes too small for the surgeon's ego—collapsed in on itself.

A NEW ROOM coalesced around them—a workroom.

Carol instantly recognized the room, with computer stations lining two walls and a couch against another. In the middle of the room sat three, rectangular plastic tables, each connected end-to-end to form a single, long table. This had been the workroom for surgical residents, and the night Carol and the Ghost of Christmas Past were visiting was Christmas Eve, some ten years earlier.

The tables were covered in plastic tablecloths, printed with bright poinsettias. Food was spread across the table, a mixture of essential Christmas nutrition, like ham, sweet potatoes, deviled eggs, bread rolls, baked mac n' cheese, stuffing, turkey, and more—all brought in by the residents and their spouses. A half-dozen or so surgical residents were in the room, some working on computers and others playing computer games.

A younger Carol entered the room, wearing scrubs and looking worn. Her face brightened at the sight of the Christmas colors and the array of food. She walked to one end of the table and started making herself up a plate.

Clay was sitting in the workroom, too, with one foot propped up, stretching between the couch and the table and blocking young Carol's path. She scowled at her male counterpart. He was a tall, broad-shouldered blond man. Looking around the room, Carol noticed none of the other female surgeons were in the room. Clay always timed his harassment for when other women weren't around.

"Only those who brought food get to dine," Clay said.

"I brought food," Carol retorted.

"Oh, yeah. What?"

"The pecan pie." Carol stepped over his leg.

"That was yours? Wasn't bad. It's store-bought though —the other girls brought homemade dishes."

Carol refrained from reminding Clay that his female colleagues were *women*, not girls. She looked at the table, noticing the even mixture of both store-bought and homemade dishes, so plenty of men must have brought store-bought food. With a sniff, she continued to prepare herself a plate of dinner.

"So," she asked, as she loaded her plate, "because we're *women*, we're supposed to cook?"

Clay shrugged, and the gesture looked kind of like a 'yes'.

Present-day Carol pursed her lips, watching her younger self shoulder the abuse.

"He always made jabs like that," she remembered.

"Makes for a negative working environment," the ghost noted in her soft, childish voice.

"Yes—and he stole cases. Our physician mentors loved Clay because he was charismatic—and *male*, like them."

"The male physicians weren't *all* like him."

Carol shook her head. "No, of course not. Clay was the exception, not the rule. I had many very good and genuinely caring coworkers."

"Still," the little girl considered, "it must have made working here feel more like a battleground."

"All the jabs—medical school, residency, and fellowship—were like death by a thousand paper cuts." Carol thought she'd formed a barrier around these toxic memories, but judging by her visceral reaction at watching her own past, she realized maybe she hadn't fully healed from these events.

Shouldn't she look back on the negativity of the past and realize how it had made her stronger? Shouldn't she reflect with quiet appreciation how these men had made her a better woman—and a better physician—because of their sexism?

Instead, Carol felt hollow.

THE ROOM HARDENED, transforming into a two-dimensional acrylic painting, before the textured brush-strokes cracked and burst, turning to fine, colored particles and blowing away to reveal a brand new scene beneath.

This time, it was of the Chicago cityscape bathed in the glow of streetlights beneath a navy night sky. Christmas decorations filled the shopfronts along the street, while exhaust fumes from the heavy traffic puffed into the cold air before being whisked away by the brutal Chicago breeze.

Carol looked around and spotted the memory she was here to witness, watching herself emerge from the same hospital she worked at now.

This memory was also from Christmas, perhaps one year after the last memory she'd witnessed. The younger version of Carol was shivering, pulling herself into a thick, woolen coat. She nestled her cream-colored hat over a head of long, dark hair and set off into the chill at a brisk pace.

Present-day Carol remembered this eventful night. She'd just finished a shift and was off for the rest of the night. Off for Christmas Eve—but back to work for Christmas night.

Young Carol walked past carolers and Christmas trees. Horse-drawn carriages, decorated with holly and blinking lights, jingled down the road carrying rosy-cheeked couples bundled together beneath blankets.

...and visions of sugarplums danced through their head.

Magic had been in the air this night—it was palpable.

Carol heard one of her favorite Christmas songs: *Baby, It's Cold Outside*. She turned to see the source of the music.

A man was standing on the street corner, painting the enormous Christmas tree at Millennium Park on a large canvas. He'd set himself up with an easel and palette, and the work he was producing was exquisite. The artist had caught every detail of the glowing lights, reminiscent of a Thomas Kinkade painting, but still distinctly different to the man who'd been described as the Painter of Light.

Younger Carol approached the artist.

"It looks beautiful," she said to the backside of the painter, "but I'm surprised your paint isn't frozen stiff." She looked at his palette.

The man turned around and smiled at her.

She'd expected the painter to be someone older, but the man appeared to be only a few years older than she'd been at the time.

"Thank you." The artist rattled his pockets. "I keep a few tubes of acrylic in here, to keep them from solidifying."

Carol shivered. "It's a little chilly to be painting outside, isn't it?"

The artist rinsed his brush. "Actually, this is the warmest Christmas Eve Chicago has had in a decade. I couldn't miss the opportunity."

He gestured toward her scrubs. "Are you coming from work? Or going there?"

"Done with work."

"That's a blessing."

Was it? Carol never really understood that phrase, and "done with work" only meant until the next shift.

"Well, your tree is fantastic. Stay warm." Carol turned to leave.

"It's almost done," the artist rushed to say. "Wouldn't you like to wait and see the finished product?"

"These scrubs are paper thin," she shivered. "I need to get warm."

"Here." The artist pulled hand warmers from his pockets and gave them to her. "Give me ten minutes to finish. If you do, I'll buy you a hot meal in a warm restaurant."

Carol opened her mouth, about to object to this presumptuous dinner invitation from a complete stranger...

...but then, he smiled.

"I'm Liam."

Oh, that smile.

Young or present-day version, it didn't matter—neither Carol had ever seen something so warm and welcoming as Liam's smile. It was, in a word, *Christmas*. His smile was a radiant, festive gift.

"Carol." She smiled in return.

As Liam resumed painting, Carol noticed his expensive shoes and the fine, leather case for his painting supplies. This was no poor street artist, yet he'd still chosen to paint outdoors, on this cold, Christmas Eve.

When Liam finished, he let Carol take a photo of him beside his masterpiece—a masterpiece which he instantly dismissed as merely mediocre.

She shook her head. So far, the man's only flaw was his perfectionism.

Together, they packed his belongings into the leather luggage bag and secured the finished painting in a tote bag.

Liam turned off the Christmas music playing on his phone and slid the device into his pocket. Then, he insisted they ride to a nearby restaurant in one of the horse-drawn carriages. Carol balked at the over-priced impracticality.

"I've never ridden in one," Liam retorted, "and it's Christmas Eve. Relax. It'll be fun."

Liam pulled her into one of the carriages. His rough textured hands were warm.

Carol then watched her younger self get carried away in the carriage, sharing a blanket with a stranger who'd smelled like cinnamon and nutmeg.

"We talked until the restaurant closed," Carol told the child ghost, standing there wistfully. "I shared everything with that man, and I'd never shared myself with anyone before."

No one before Liam, and no one since he'd left.

"You still love him," the ghost said matter-of-factly.

Carol sniffed and bundled her robe tighter around her body. She couldn't feel the frigid chill from the night of this memory, but she felt cold nonetheless.

Five

The buildings and storefronts, adorned with their Christmas lights, blurred into a hazy Monet watercolor—before finally washing away completely to reveal bright, white lights.

As Carol blinked at the offending harsh light, an operating room came into focus around her, towering white walls and a sterile glow surrounding them. Beams of light concentrated on the exposed abdomen of a patient in the middle of surgery.

Carol watched a version of herself—this one in full sterile attire of gown, gloves, cap, and mask—assist a robust, older surgeon with a colon resection.

Present-day Carol's brain worked out from when this

memory originated. She was observing herself as a resident, not long after having met Liam. Young Carol was no longer a medical student who watched from a distance or held retractors. She was directly contributing to this operation, moving intestines and suctioning blood. When the surgery eventually finished, Carol would be allowed to suture the abdomen shut.

The particular surgeon she'd been operating alongside that night was harsh. His hands moved fast with the practice of many years. He barked orders at Carol, and if she didn't move fast enough, he'd 'inadvertently' poke her with a needle and then blame her for it.

Carol remembered that her first surgeries with this surgeon had landed her three needle sticks and a series of blood tests in the weeks that followed, all to make sure she hadn't contracted any diseases from the patients.

Every surgical resident—male and female—knew the hazard of working with this surgeon, but everyone was too afraid to report his behavior. In hindsight, Carol suspected that if a half-dozen surgical residents had banded together to report him, the medical center would have been forced to investigate. Maybe not, though, if the whistleblowers had all been women.

"I hated him." Carol seethed as her chill from earlier was replaced by heated anger.

Her blood boiled as she stood once again in the same OR as this egotistical, maniacal surgeon, watching her terrified younger self try to help, while avoiding injury.

Carol knew this painful trip down memory lane was supposed to be a lesson, so she pre-empted the Ghost of

Christmas Past by clarifying: "I've never been, and never will be, anything like *him*."

How many times had this surgeon brought her to tears by making her feel inferior? Too slow. Too sloppy. How many times had he mumbled 'damn, worthless surgeon' when they'd worked together?

Carol shook with rage at the memory of it.

"You're not like him," the ghost agreed. "Not yet."

The operating room faded to black.

A FAINT GLOW of green and red lit an entirely different room. A Christmas tree came into focus. Carol looked around and instantly recognized the room. It was the apartment she'd once shared with Liam.

The small apartment had a tiny gas fireplace, lit specially for the occasion, and the tree stood in one corner. Above the fireplace, the television was set to play Christmas music on repeat.

It wasn't Christmas, exactly, Carol recalled. She'd had to work December 23 through to December 27, so she and Liam were celebrating on December 28 instead.

Her younger self danced around the room wearing a low-cut, red velvet pajama set. Liam wore candy cane-covered flannel pajama pants—and nothing else.

"I love it! I love it!" Carol—Santa Carol, in those pajamas—exclaimed happily.

She gazed on the Christmas present Liam had given her —a stunning painting of human lungs with Liam's signature, artistic flare. He'd rendered the airway branches to look like the boughs of a tree, and the image was vividly life-like with blue and green leaves and breathtaking depth and shadow.

The timing of the gift had coincided with her acceptance into cardiothoracic surgery fellowship. Tears spilled down Carol's cheeks—both past-Carol and present-day Carol. Liam took the Santa-adorned Carol into his arms and kissed her passionately.

He'd been so passionate.

His hands worked their way under her shirt as they kissed their way to the couch. She ran her hands along his bare chest as he laughed and tumbled on top of her.

"I love you, Liam."

Present-day Carol reached out a hand and covered the ghost child's eyes. The spirit might be centuries older than her ghostly appearance suggested, but she still didn't need to see what had happened next.

Eventually, Carol recalled, she and Liam had returned to gift giving, and Liam opened the new set of brushes she'd bought him.

Present-day Carol turned back to stare at Liam's painting of the lung-tree. She still had that painting to this day. She'd carefully wrapped it up and stored it in her closet, because it had become too painful to look at. The beautiful painting was a reminder of what she'd lost—what she'd let go.

OBJECTS SHIFTED and shimmered around them, and then the same apartment went fast-forward two years into the future.

Young Carol and Liam were arguing.

With a wave of nausea, present-day Carol remembered this fight—their last fight. Ever.

With raised voices, the two of them had bickered about a familiar topic: Carol was spending too much time at work, and Liam was feeling neglected.

"You're never home, Carol."

"I have a job, Liam."

"A job that means more to you than I do!"

Present-day Carol tuned out the painful exchange of words. Regardless of the excuses she'd made—career advancement, being better than the competition, and being needed by patients—enough time had passed since this last fight for her to reflect, ruminate, and accept the truth behind the excuses.

"I don't want to see this," Carol told the ghost beside her. "I've already been through the pain of it once."

Once—and a thousand more times, as she'd replayed this memory over the years. She'd replayed it so many times, it was redundant to watch it yet again.

The truth was that Carol had never had anybody love her as completely as Liam had, and she'd never been able to bring herself to feel as though she deserved him.

Carol never felt worthy of his love.

"You're smothering me!" Young Carol was shouting at Liam.

Carol cringed at the sound of her own words. When she saw the crushed look on Liam's face, her heart felt like it was breaking all over again. She collapsed to her knees, clutching her stomach.

"Stop," she begged the little girl. "Please, make it stop. Why are you showing me this? I can't change the past."

"The past cannot be changed," the redhead replied, "but it doesn't have to be repeated."

"I don't want to repeat it. That's why I never went back to him."

"There's another way," the voice of the small ghost trailed off, and then she vanished.

CAROL WIPED away tears and looked up.

As she composed herself, she looked around. She was kneeling on the floor of her brownstone, surrounded by the familiar, soft gray walls. Her heart pounded with a dull ache.

In panicked haste, she reached for her phone and dialed Liam's number.

Did he even still have the same number?

The call went straight to voicemail.

"Liam, it's Carol," her words came out rushed. "I just..."

Her voice trailed off. What did she want? She just wanted to hear his voice, but that seemed like a ridiculous thing to say. Instead, Carol finished her message: "I just wanted to wish you a Merry Christmas. It was good to see you today."

Still on the line, Carol forced herself to take a deep breath. As she did so, she looked up and caught sight of the clock on the wall.

1:45 a.m.

She bit back a groan. How inappropriate to call Liam so late! Could she delete the voicemail? Possibly, but he'd still see that she'd called.

"...and don't sell the horse painting—*please*."

With that, Carol disconnected the call.

She tossed the phone aside and deflated back to the floor. She felt empty, like her insides had been scooped out, and the little girl had been just the first of her scheduled supernatural visitors.

How much time until the next ghost arrived to further emotionally torture her?

Carol had thought she'd effectively buried the past, but now the memories were back—fresh and raw after the Ghost of Christmas Past had forced her to revisit them.

The pain now felt days old, rather than dulled by the passing years. Carol had forgotten how much she'd distanced herself from these memories, and that wasn't the only thing.

She thought of Melanie. She'd distanced herself from her sister, too. They'd been so close once.

And Liam. Carol had forgotten how hard she'd pushed him away. He'd been so loving that she'd felt inadequate in her reciprocation, but instead of trying harder, her response had been to distance herself from him.

Could she ever be the compassionate older sister that Melanie deserved? Or the doting companion in a balanced relationship? Could Carol rediscover that side of herself? Or was that a gorge too far to cross?

She stumbled to the bathroom and splashed cold water on her face. Staring at herself in the mirror, Carol brushed the tangles out of her dark, shoulder-length hair. In her reflection, her brown eyes looked tired and her cheekbones pale.

She took a deep breath and stood up straight. Then,

with determination, Carol strode into the bedroom and changed into blue jeans and a forest green sweater. She might not have any choice about being dragged around Chicago by supernatural entities, but she didn't have to be wearing a silk robe as she did so.

When Carol walked into the kitchen to get herself a glass of water, she froze.

A burly, bald man in torn overalls and stained work boots was standing there.

Were it not for his green sweater—with Rudolf sporting a flashing red nose on it—Carol might have thought this new arrival was a burglar. The ghostly stranger grinned at her, and she relaxed somewhat. His smile was encased in a shaggy beard of gray, wiry hair—but it was warm and genuine.

"I'm the Ghost of Christmas Present."

"You look more like a janitor," she responded coolly. "I'm Carol, your next victim."

The ghost gave a hearty laugh, one that seemed to reverberate throughout the room. The warmth of his mirth even spread through Carol, dispelling the cold clinging to her after watching her wretched past.

"Shall we begin?" The spirit's voice was a deep baritone.

"Lead the way," Carol answered, devoid of enthusiasm.

The Ghost of Christmas Present led Carol through a doorway, one that had materialized where her refrigerator had once been.

Carol found herself standing in a tiny apartment, decorated festively with a small tree and a string of lights stretched across the border between the walls and ceiling. A bald-headed boy sat in front of the tree, beneath which lay a solitary present.

Carol walked forward, confident that the hairless boy couldn't see or hear her. She observed the paleness of his skin and the dark bruises on his arms.

"Cancer?"

"Unfortunately, yes," the Ghost of Christmas Present replied. "Leukemia."

"Whose son is he?"

"Corey, let's do this!" The answer came in the sound of a cheerful voice. Carol's physician assistant, Johnny, walked into the room wearing blue and white snowflake decorated cotton pajamas and black slippers.

Carol glanced at the shoes by the door to the apartment. They were the same, worn loafers she'd been annoyed at day after day—hanging beneath the familiar, elbow-shredded white coat of her physician assistant.

Johnny's wife entered the room, looking tired, but with a warm smile on her face at seeing her son by the tree. "Open it, Corey."

The boy tore into the present.

"Only one?" Carol asked.

The ghost didn't reply.

"An Xbox!" Corey's face lit with a smile. He stopped before opening the box. "But you said it would cost too much, because we needed to cover the cost of chemo."

Johnny rubbed the top of his head. "I got a bonus."

Carol choked at the lie. A lump of coal hit her stomach like a rock dropping into a well.

She didn't set Johnny's salary—that was done by the hospital—but she knew his wages were in the bottom third of the national average. Someone with his level of experience and dedication ought to make a lot more.

Carol glanced at the Ghost of Christmas Present.

"I can talk to administration—argue for a raise." Her voice was a dry whisper.

"You said it yourself," the ghost responded, "the insured have the highest amount of medical debt. Johnny earns enough that he simultaneously doesn't qualify for medical financial assistance, but also can't cover the large deductible and out-of-pocket expenses for his son's treatment."

Carol gulped dryly. "I'll talk to administration about getting him a bonus, too."

The ghost nodded, stroking his beard.

The boy's mother came back into the small living room and handed Corey a mug of hot chocolate.

"Thanks, Mom. Thanks for the gift! I'm going to set it up!"

As Corey went to the television, Johnny and his wife—Penny—moved to the kitchen. Carol tried to remember if she'd ever actually met Penny. No, she decided. She knew the name from Johnny mentioning her, but Penny had never come to see her husband at work, at least not while Carol had been around.

"You didn't get a bonus," Penny snapped at him.

"I know," Johnny nodded. "I just wanted to make him happy."

"Ugh." Penny groaned. "It's that horrible woman you work for. You need to find a better job."

Johnny kept his voice low. "We've been over this. Corey's best medical care is here in Chicago, and I can't work anywhere else in the city with my noncompete clause."

Penny lowered her head and stepped into his arms. "I know. I'm sorry. Let's just make this the best Christmas we can for Corey."

Goosebumps prickled Carol's arms. Why the best? Had they been told this would be his last?

"Is Corey going to be okay?" Carol turned to the ghost, a pleading, shaky edge to her voice.

"I can't see the future," he replied dryly. "Only the present."

Six

The lights on Johnny's Christmas tree blurred, and a different living room, filled with a blue and white Christmas tree, slowly came into focus.

Melanie came into view, wearing the same festive colors from when Carol had seen her earlier, back when it had still been Christmas Eve. Carol stood in the living room of her younger sister's two-bedroomed loft.

The live Christmas tree was so plush that it filled one entire corner of the room and stretched so tall that the silver star brushed against the ceiling. Stockings hung over the gas-lit fireplace—four in all, each made from soft green and red velvet material. *Oh, Holy Night* played through a speaker system, while the couch was covered with

Christmas pillows in vibrant gold and silver. Charles Dickens's *A Christmas Carol* sat in hardback on the mahogany coffee table.

As she stood there, Carol's sister held a framed photo, her expression uncharacteristically doleful. Melanie's husband, Pike, came into the room wearing red and green flannel pajamas. He towered over Melanie's small frame and wrapped gentle arms around her waist from behind.

Pike looked over Melanie's shoulder.

"The party was great. I'm sorry your sister didn't show."

"It was great." Melanie sighed. "I was hoping to give Carol her gift."

Carol peered closer at the framed photo in Melanie's hands.

A Christmas long ago was captured beneath the glass. In the picture, Carol was sixteen and had one arm slung over an eleven-year-old Melanie. They both wore Santa hats and broad smiles.

Carol swallowed and stepped back, watching Melanie gingerly tuck the photo in a decorative box and cushion it in white tissue paper.

"I wanted to tell her about..." Melanie's voice trailed off, and her hand lowered to her abdomen.

Carol looked back at the four stockings over the fireplace—one for Melanie, one for Pike, and one each for...

"Oh, Mel!" Carol's heart swelled with excitement for her little sister's expanding family. "She's pregnant!"

When Carol looked to the ghost for confirmation, he nodded.

"Twins?"

He laughed heartily. "Yes. Fortune has fallen upon them double-fold."

Carol smiled. "Thank you for showing me this, Spirit. I want to be a part of their lives. I want to be the best aunt they'll ever have."

"You'll be the *only* aunt they'll ever have." His eyes twinkled.

She nudged him with her elbow playfully, surprised that she could physically touch this supernatural entity. "You know what I mean."

With a swell of excitement, Carol looked back at her sister.

A BEEPING OF MACHINES SOUNDED, intruding on Carol's pleasant thoughts. Around her and the Ghost of Christmas Present, Melanie's apartment faded, replaced by a sterile ICU room. The beeping came from a monitor by a patient's bed, which showing a steady heartbeat and stable blood pressure. The ventilator supplied timed, incremental breaths through a breathing tube.

"Mr. Johnson." Carol let out an anguished sigh.

She looked at the ghost, whose bald head seemed to reflect the bright, fluorescent lights of the ICU room.

"I did what I could," Carol told him. "I tried to help him. He tolerated the surgery, but his lungs were too weak to come off the ventilator. Then, he contracted pneumonia."

The Ghost of Christmas Present dipped his head. "And his crime of failing to recover should doom him to being on life support? Which delays his inevitable death?"

"He isn't in pain," she replied. Mr. Johnson was comfortable on intravenous sedatives.

The large ghost motioned toward two women in the room, who sat in chairs watching over their loved one. Their drooping eyes and anguished expressions spoke volumes—a visual demonstration as to the extent of their suffering.

Carol raked her fingernails through her hair. "It's not my fault. Surgeons are graded based on their thirty-day mortality rate. If I pull the plug, I'm affecting my numbers —which, in the future, will only hurt other patients who…"

She stopped when she heard the quiet sobs of Mr. Johnson's wife.

Carol paced the room. "Okay, okay, I get it. These are people, not numbers. You've made your point, Spirit. Can we go now?"

The ghost hooked his thumbs through the straps of his overalls. The ICU room shimmered before transforming into a two-dimensional, vividly textured acrylic painting. The painting turned from the gloomy scene of a patient in a hospital bed to that of a beach at sunset.

The palm trees in the painting appeared so life-like that a real breeze might have made the painted leaves move.

Carol didn't have to look at the artist's name to know whose work this was.

Liam.

She knew those brush strokes. She knew the hands that had crafted this masterpiece.

As Carol watched, she saw Liam standing there—beside an elderly man who leaned on a cane. They both wore tuxedos, and Carol recognized the room as part of the gallery she'd visited on Christmas Eve. Side by side, the two men stared at the shimmering water of the painting.

"Have you ever loved something you couldn't have?" The old man asked that of Liam without turning his gaze from the textured rendition of water.

"Indeed I have, Mr. Moretti."

"Sometimes, the pain of it feels like a trickling bleed," the old man mused. "An ache that slowly, subtly takes your life."

"You're not wrong, sir." Liam moved to clasp his hands behind his back. "This will be my last auction, Mr. Moretti."

Shock registered on Mr. Moretti's face. "But you've done so well, Liam! The fund raiser has been stupendous, year after year."

"My heart isn't in it anymore. I apologize."

"What will you do?"

"Perhaps I need time. Perhaps I need to find a way to stop the hemorrhaging."

"Oh, Liam." Carol wanted to reach for him—to comfort him—but they were on such different paths now, weren't they?

If she didn't think she deserved Liam *then*, she certainly didn't deserve him *now*.

"I don't know how to fix us," she told the spirit. "To fix *me*."

The Ghost of Christmas Present turned to her. "If he's the one giving the love, and you're the recipient of it, isn't it up to *him* to decide if you're worthy of his affection?"

Carol looked at the ghost through blurred eyes. Her temple began to throb. This was suddenly too much—just *too* much. She couldn't solve the problems of the medical community, or mend all broken relationships. She was just one person.

Another painting of Liam's popped into her head. This one was a sphere of silver spinning on a lilac-colored lake beneath a teal sky. It was a painting he'd called *The Sphere of Influence*.

Everyone had their own sphere, Liam had explained to her—their own group of people, and their own environment, which they impacted both positively and negatively.

Whenever he got overwhelmed at all of the problems of the world, Liam had said he'd remind himself to scale his concerns down to his sphere of influence, who and what he could realistically improve without damaging or overwhelming his own psyche.

Maybe Carol could do that.

She couldn't change the dysfunctional, fractured medical system in this country, but she could change how she navigated through it.

The system might reward delayed, assembly-line care, but she didn't have to conform to that. Carol could add her own compassion at no cost to her. She could have a positive impact in her sphere of influence, even if nowhere else.

"I think I can do it. I think I know how to change."

The ghost gave Carol a beaming smile, and then he began to fade from the gallery.

"Then, you're already on your way to success," his voice lingered after him.

"Thank you for showing me the present."

The ghost dipped his head as he vanished.

. . .

CAROL FOUND herself alone in the art gallery.

She stepped forward, wandering through the gallery until she vaguely noticed the scenery change around her. She blinked, shaking her head and looking around the new location.

She found herself in an apartment again, standing in a dark, unwelcoming living room.

In one corner, a towering figure, utterly unmoving and wearing a long, dark hood.

A chill ran down her spine and Carol shuddered at the sight of the Ghost of Christmas Future—Christmas Yet to Come.

He might as well be Death himself, or perhaps he was, because death was the inevitable outcome awaiting everyone.

Carol looked around the apartment again, fearing whose it might be—and what terrible future this ghost intended to show her.

Then, she saw them.

Johnny and his wife, crying together as they held a photograph of Corey in their hands.

Finally, Carol recognized the tiny apartment. It was theirs—but devoid of Christmas decorations, unlike the last time she'd seen it.

Carol's chest tightened. Surely, this hadn't happened—or didn't *have* to happen. This was a vision of the future, after all, and the future hadn't happened yet.

Corey just needed appropriate and timely treatment, that was all.

"No, no, no."

Carol spun away from the heart-breaking scene—only to find herself back on the cold, dark streets of Chicago. This winter snow fell from a bleak sky, heavy with dark clouds.

She whirled around, back to face the Ghost of Christmas Yet to Come.

"Stop it! That won't happen. I won't *let* it happen."

The enormous, cloaked figure said nothing. He only pointed a long, bony finger. Carol's gaze followed the direction he indicated.

She wiped tears out of her eyes and focused on a scraggly, weather-beaten man huddled in an oversized, stained coat. He was leaning against the wall of an abandoned storefront, with an unshaven beard and dirt-caked fingernails. His eyes looked distant and destitute.

Two women stopped to stare at him before continuing on their walk.

"I heard he was a famous painter, until he stopped painting one day." One of the women whispered to the other, her voice audible as the women passed where Carol was standing. "He traded his brushes for booze until he went broke..."

Carol shook her head, turning back to the homeless man. She recognized him through the dark beard; although not as the man she'd seen on Christmas Eve.

"No," Carol breathed. "Not Liam."

She turned back to the ghost, desperately grabbing hold of his abundant black robes. She looked up into the void of his faceless black hood.

"It doesn't have to be this way," Carol pleaded. "Let me

fix it. I can save him—the way he saved me."

Carol turned toward the homeless man—her Liam.

She reached him, kneeling down to touch his bundled figure...

...and, instead, falling straight through the now-intangible sidewalk.

Carol screamed, plummeting into nothing. She fell through the darkness and landed roughly on her hands and knees, kneeling in soft dirt.

She struggled up to her feet, spinning around to face walls of dirt in every direction. Then, she looked up—at the rim of the six-foot deep hole she'd fallen into.

Looming down above her, she saw a tombstone.

DR. CAROL SULLIVAN

Above her on one side stood the large, hooded figure.

On the other stood Johnny, dressed in a black suit with Penny beside him.

High above, a gray sky hung heavy with clouds. Down in the pit—her own grave—Carol felt frigid with fear.

"Why did we come here?" Penny asked, looming over Carol's grave.

"Somebody had to," Johnny replied. "After all, she was my boss. She helped some people."

"As long as she was helping herself."

Johnny didn't refute that. Instead, he looked down into the grave and murmured: "Goodbye, Carol."

Then, the couple turned and walked away from her grave, leaving Carol alone in the darkness.

She wasn't alone for long. Someone else approached. Carol looked up and saw her sister standing at the edge of the grave.

She gulped.

Melanie didn't look much older than she was now, which meant...

Carol turned and looked up at the looming, black figure of Christmas Yet to Come. She longed to ask him: "When is this supposed to happen?"

But she knew he wouldn't answer her—and, in truth, she didn't need him to. She knew the answer.

Soon, apparently.

With tears in her eyes, Melanie dropped a single, red rose into the grave. It fell, landing in the dirt at Carol's feet —the pedals scattering their crimson colors, in contrast to the black earth beneath them.

When Melanie left, someone began shoveling dirt into the grave.

Carol pressed herself against one wall of moist dirt as more cascaded down around her.

"Mel," she called up, out of the grave. "Mel, wait! Come back!"

Carol then turned toward the other side of the grave, where the Ghost of Christmas Yet to Come and his shabby black cloak towered over her. She tried to claw her way out of the deep, dark hole, but she couldn't find purchase in the moist dirt.

"Wait!" she cried. "I know what I have to do! I know how to change! Please!" She slipped and fell, landing on her back with a thud.

The dirt kept coming. Shovel-load after shovel-load, scooped up with the grating of metal against dirt.

"No!" Carol screamed.

Then, all fell silent.

Seven

Carol opened her eyes.

She was lying on her back in her bed, tangled in her bedsheets and still wearing her jeans and sweater.

I'm alive.

She scrambled to the edge of the bed and snatched her phone off the charging station.

6 A.M. DECEMBER 25

Christmas day!

She stumbled out of bed and across the hallway into her home office. There, she logged onto her computer. In rapid succession, she sent several emails. Then, she ordered precooked entrees and sides to be delivered in the afternoon.

Next, she found the gallery website where Liam's work was showcased.

After making her purchases, Carol dashed to the bathroom, feeling like she was floating on a cloud of elation. She was alive—so full of life—and she knew what she needed to do.

After freshening up, she grabbed her purse and hospital badge. Standing on the curb outside her brownstone, Carol inhaled crisp, chill air—the best kind, after a fresh snowfall. She caught a cab to the hospital.

En route, she called Jeff, one of the hospital financial officers.

"Carol, it's Christmas day." His voice crackled with irritation and exasperation. "Is there some financial crisis at the hospital?"

"Merry Christmas, Jeff."

"Uh, Merry Christmas," he replied uncertainly.

"I need a Christmas miracle," Carol said firmly. "Johnny has been my physician assistant for five years. He needs a Christmas bonus—a good one. That, and a raise—effective January 1st. He's underpaid, based on national averages, factoring in his experience and the cost of living for Chicago."

"You're telling me this now? Today?"

"A Christmas miracle, Jeff. I need you to make this happen."

"Carol..." he started to protest.

"Don't give me the company line about budget cuts and lean margins," Carol cut him off. "We've underpaid Johnny for far too long. Whenever he figures that out, he'll leave us for a job that pays him what he's worth. If I lose

Johnny, my work productivity will fall by half until we hire and train a replacement. We both know that's a six to twelve-month endeavor, which is a much bigger loss than treating our employees as they ought to be treated."

"Okay, okay," Jeff sighed, "I can do the raise by January, but I can't release bonus funds on a holiday."

"I'll get him the bonus, and you can reimburse me," Carol replied. "I'm also doing one pro-bono case per month, starting in January."

"Carol..."

"Get behind it, Jeff. I'll get key administrators in a meeting after the holidays. They can spin it for marketing promotion if they want, but it's happening."

"What's gotten in to you, Carol? I thought you despised Christmas."

"I found the Christmas spirit I'd lost." She paused. "Oh, and I'm not working Christmas next year." Then, she hung up the phone, paid the cab fair, and bounded into the hospital.

Alive! Carol felt positively alive!

She passed nurses, aides, and other physicians—greeting them all with a "Merry Christmas!" Some stared in shock, while others smiled and returned the wish for a pleasant holiday.

Carol walked into Mr. Smith's room. He was sitting on the edge of his bed, eating breakfast in his faded, blue hospital gown.

"Mr. Smith, you're looking well."

"Dr. Sullivan!" His unshaven face brightened. "Visiting on Christmas day?"

"I wanted to see how you're feeling. Your surgery went

well, and I see your chest tube is out now. We should be able to get you home today."

"Today? That'd be a great Christmas present! The grandkids were hoping to visit this evening."

After a few minutes of socializing, Carol bid Mr. Smith a good day.

Next, she went to the ICU. When she reached Mr. Johnson's room, she found his family—wife and daughter—seated in his room. Carol pulled up a chair and sat in front of them.

"Dr. Sullivan?" the wife asked, startled.

Carol leaned forward looked deep into Mrs. Johnson's glistening eyes.

"I'm so sorry this happened to your husband."

"You told us pneumonia could happen."

"I know," Carol nodded, "but I wish this surgery would have worked for him."

"He hoped so, too, but he didn't want to live barely able to breathe. He'd rather die trying to get a better quality of life than live struggling the way he was."

Carol nodded. Mr. Johnson had told her the same thing before his operation, and she'd been honest about the risks of the surgery.

"I'm sorry it didn't work," Carol repeated. "I'm sorry he didn't recover—that he won't recover."

"He didn't want to linger on life support."

"I know. Whenever you're ready, we'll let him pass comfortably."

Mrs. Johnson gave a pained sigh. "He's ready. Let's let the grandchildren say goodbye tomorrow. After Christmas —tomorrow."

"Tomorrow," Carol echoed. "I'll be here, and we'll do it together."

AFTER CAROL LEFT THE HOSPITAL, she grabbed a cab and stopped briefly at a department store on the way to Johnny's apartment.

With gift bag in hand, she slid out of the cab. "Keep the meter running," she called to the driver, before bounding up the stairs and knocking on Johnny's door.

Johnny answered the door in his pajamas, holding a cup of coffee. His eyes widened when he saw her. "Dr. Sullivan?"

"Merry Christmas, Johnny." She handed him the sparkling, silver bag.

"Johnny? Who's there?" Penny came to the door. At the sight of Carol, her expression darkened.

"Honey," Johnny said quickly, "Dr. Sullivan brought us a Christmas gift—isn't that *nice* of her?"

Penny's expression softened into confusion.

Carol extended a hand. "I'm Carol. We've never met, and that's inexcusable on my part."

Johnny pulled the card out of the bag and passed the bag to Penny.

"That's your bonus, Johnny," Carol explained, as he opened it. "That, and back payment on prior Christmas bonuses. There's also a letter in there, outlining your raise, effective January 1st."

Johnny stood there, eyes wide.

Carol turned to Penny.

"In the bag are a few Xbox games, and a gift card for

more games for Corey. Penny, I bought you some scarves—because we don't know each other well enough for me to know what you like, but I hope to change that."

Johnny opened the envelope and gasped at the number on the check inside.

"Penny, look at this."

He showed it to her. Her mouth fell open.

Carol backed away toward the door.

"I have to go—more deliveries to make—but I hope you'll come this evening to my house for Christmas dinner. The invitation should be in your email."

Carol then turned and scurried down the stairs. She nearly tripped on the bottom one, catching herself and laughing at her own clumsiness.

Once back in the cab, she directed the driver to Melanie's apartment.

The cab pulled up, and Carol paid the driver. She grabbed her bag and strode into the apartment complex.

When Carol knocked on the door to her sister's apartment, Pike answered—with disheveled morning hair and stubble on his jaw.

He scratched his chin. "Carol? This is a pleasant surprise. Come on in."

Carol stepped inside, dropping the gift bag on the floor. She hugged her brother-in-law, and his posture stiffened in surprise.

"Thank you for being so good to Mel," Carol breathed, pressing her head against his broad chest.

"Carol?" Melanie walked into the room, eyes widening.

"Mel!" Carol's heart soared to see her sister. She rushed

to hug her, and, just as quickly, she spun around and picked up the gift bag, thrusting it toward her sister.

"I bought baby stuff," Carol explained. "All gender neutral—but it's a start." Her eyes sparkled. "And I bought two of everything."

Melanie's eyes widened even further. "But how could you *possibly* know?"

Carol didn't answer. Instead, she continued: "And if you're not otherwise engaged, come to my Christmas dinner tonight." Then, Carol hugged Melanie again. "It's so good to see you."

With that, Carol abruptly turned and headed toward the door. She had one more stop to make before going back to her house to prepare for Christmas dinner.

"Wait!" Melanie ran after her, snatching a small box from under her tree. "Take your gift, but we *will* see you later, too."

Carol graciously accepted the box, which she recognized instantly.

She smiled but didn't open the gift.

"Thank you, Mel. It's one of my favorite photos. A perfect gift."

Leaving the couple pleasantly flabbergasted, Carol strode out of their apartment building and down the stairs to the street.

She pulled her coat tighter around her and breathed the air in deeply one more time. She'd go to The Stardust Gallery next, hoping to find Liam—*if* he checked his email and *if* he wanted to show up.

. . .

TEN MINUTES LATER, a cab dropped Carol outside the gallery. She walked up to the door, but could already see through the glass that the lights were off.

Well, it was mid-morning on Christmas, so perhaps Liam hadn't checked his email after all. Alternatively—and sadly, more probable—he just didn't want to see her.

She couldn't blame him.

Carol tested the door. Locked. She peered inside and saw no movement within.

Turning, Carol walked back toward the street, one foot in front of the other. She was within walking distance of her brownstone now, but the need to see Liam overwhelmed her.

There was so much to make up for. She didn't know if he'd ever forgive her but she needed to try.

Cars zipped up and down the street. Carol neared the curb.

She swallowed and resolved not to give up on what she and Liam had. She'd check her email and see if he replied. Perhaps he had, and perhaps they could set up another rendezvous.

Still, as Carol pulled her phone from her pocket, she couldn't help but feel disappointment worm its way into her mind.

She reached the curb and extended her right leg to step down...

"Carol!" A cheerful male voice called to her.

Carol turned, paused mid-step. Then, she pulled her foot back and turned toward the sound of the voice—Liam.

As she pivoted toward him, a delivery truck barreled

past her on the road—buffeting her and blasting cold air through her hair.

At the sight of Liam's smile, Carol barely even noticed the gush of wind from the truck hurtling past her. Instead, she walked toward him—barely resisting the urge to run into his arms.

Liam wore a cream-colored sweater and a fur-lined leather jacket. His dark hair was combed sleekly back, and his dark eyes twinkled with something like anticipation.

"Are you the 6 a.m. buyer, by any chance?"

"Yes," Carol grinned. "I *had* to have it."

In addition to sending several emails that morning, Carol had also finally purchased the horse painting—and a few others from the online store of The Stardust Gallery.

Liam smiled at her. "You lost sleep over it?"

She swallowed. "I lost sleep over you." A sense of vulnerability closed around her. The way she'd treated him, Liam had every right to lash out at her now.

"Over *me*?"

"Over *us*," she amended, her voice shaky. "I never should have let you go, Liam. Can you forgive me?"

His lips parted in a welcoming smile. "Carol, I forgave you the moment I saw you desperate to open the gallery doors on Christmas morning."

She leaned closer, arched up, and kissed him.

The kiss was as wonderful as she'd remembered—sweet and sensual, delicious and delightful, heavenly and homecoming. His kiss was Christmas—magical and miraculous.

When they broke away, she no longer felt cold and her loneliness melted away.

"What changed?" Liam asked, tucking her into his arms.

"Everything."

Tony sat on Carol's counter, unseen by all as he watched Christmas dinner unfold at her home. He'd only been granted that one moment to speak to her, when Carol had seen him on Christmas Eve. That would never happen again, according to the Christmas Spirits. Considering how badly he'd scared her, it was probably a good thing.

Tonight, he couldn't help but grin at the sight of so much holiday cheer. Carol's dining room was filled with green, red, and gold decorations—candles, miniature trees, and napkins. The table bowed beneath a Christmas turkey, green beans, mashed potatoes, buttered bread rolls, cranberry sauce, cornbread stuffing, and more. Tony wished he could smell all those delicious scents, mixed with the pumpkin pie baking in the oven.

Melanie, Pike, and Penny were busy bringing serving spoons to the table—while Johnny poured wine into waiting glasses. Corey snuck a bread roll while no one was looking.

In the kitchen, Liam and Carol couldn't keep their hands off each other. Carol couldn't stop smiling. Tony had never seen her so happy.

"Mission accomplished," Burke said, shimmering into manifestation beside Tony.

"Better than that," Tony grinned. "She's happy, changed, *and* still alive."

"The spirit of Christmas wins again, thanks to the Christmas Spirits."

"I got my Christmas miracle," Tony beamed.

"That you did."

Tony looked down at his arms and legs. "Whoa! What's happening?" He was growing even more translucent than he already was.

"You're moving on, Tony," Burke smiled. "Your spirit is at peace."

"Oh? Great! Wait." Tony's eyes widened. "What about you?"

"I've got my own unfinished business. Don't worry about me."

"See you in the next world, Burke?"

"See you, Tony."

One Year Later

Carol fluffed the pillows and poured the wine, excited for Liam's arrival home. He was finishing up at the gallery charity auction and was due back at any moment.

His painting of the horses hung above the fireplace. To his delight, she'd redecorated her brownstone living room last January to match the colors and beauty of the painting.

Rediscovering their love had happened so seamlessly that they were already married come springtime. They'd honeymooned in Alaska. Carol had then cut back her work hours to a normal, full-time load—and she now spent most weeknights and weekends with her husband. They sailed

Lake Michigan, walked through the parks together, and kissed at every opportunity, as if they were teenagers, instead of in their forties.

Melanie had given birth to two adorable twin girls—and soon after, Carol had begun making time to give the new mom a regular weekend break, babysitting for a few hours so Melanie could indulge in some much-needed self-care.

Meanwhile, Pike spoiled the twins with every female superhero outfit and action figure he could find, which was a lot of them.

Corey had finished cancer treatments, and his last bone marrow biopsy showed complete remission. Johnny and Penny had dinner with Carol and Liam once a month. Usually, the men cooked while Carol and Penny had long discussions over what wine paired best with the food.

When Carol heard the door unlocking, she walked over to greet Liam. He entered with a flourish, spinning her in a circle with one hand wrapped around her waist, and a hungry kiss pressed against her lips. He pulled her against him as he spun her around, still kissing her senseless.

"Liam," Carol said breathlessly, between kisses, "what's in your other hand?"

Reluctantly, he pulled away.

"Your Christmas gift," he pulled his arm behind his back, "but I know when I give it to you, you're going to neglect me, so I had to get my affections in first."

"What is it?" She laughed, trying to peek around to see what he had hidden behind his back.

Liam surrendered and thrust a squirming ball of fur at her.

"I'm not sure what he is—some type of mutt. He's a rescue, and the newest member of our family."

Carol sunk both hands into the puppy's soft, golden fur. He waggled an excited tail.

"He's adorable!" Carol inspected him as she petted the squirming pup. "Definitely some Terrier. Maybe miniature Poodle and Schnauzer mix?"

Liam brought the puppy close to his face, and they nuzzled noses. "I think adorable covers it."

Carol took the puppy in her hands, and he licked them enthusiastically. "He's wonderful."

"What should we name him?"

"Something that's *us*," she pondered. "We met at Michigan Avenue—the Christmas tree."

"By Wrigley Square."

Carol smiled. "Wrigley!"

Liam grinned and leaned in for another kiss. "Wrigley? I like that."

"Come here, you." She tugged Liam closer—until there was no space between their bodies. "I'll never neglect you."

"Really? Let's have that glass of wine—and then you spend the night not neglecting me."

"I can do that."

Liam dipped his head for another kiss. "I love you."

"I love you, too."

<<<<<>>>>>

BRIEF NOTE FROM THE AUTHOR:

Are you in the mood for more holiday adventure?
Grab Holly's Holiday or Stella's Star. You can also get all three in Samet's **Christmas Collection**

<h1 style="text-align:center">Dear Reader</h1>

If you enjoyed this book and want to know about future releases by CB Samet you can visit www.cbsamet.com to sign up for my mailing list! I promise I won't spam you. I only send an email when I have a new book released, giveaways, or special discounts. And I'll never sell your information. You can also unsubscribe at any time.

You can also click the link below to follow me on BookBub.

Keep reading to get to a sample chapter at the end of this book!

Also, as an author, I rely heavily on readers to spread the word about books they've read. If you enjoyed this story, kindly let others know by posing a brief comment on social media or leave a review where you purchased it.

Thank you for reading,
CB Samet

Bonus

EXCERPT FROM HOLLY'S HOLIDAY

Drex sat down on the park bench. "African swallow or European swallow?"

"Doesn't matter. A swallow cannot carry a coconut." The man beside him on the bench pushed his glasses up on his nose as he shifted his weight in the chair. Ludvik's English was good for never having lived outside the Czech Republic.

"I divided information. Some on phone and some on USB," Ludvik said.

Drex withdrew his phone and laid it on his thigh. The man did the same.

As the data transferred, Ludvik dabbed a handkerchief to his forehead, despite the cool air around them. "When do I get immunity?"

"The information needs to be verified, and then the US government will be in touch."

"You're not the US government?" Ludvik's voice raised an octave in surprise.

"I'm just the middleman." Drex kept his gaze scanning his surroundings—Letná Park was beautiful despite the bare trees of November. A pale blue sky held wisps of white clouds. A breeze dropped the wind chill to around forty degrees. Birds flocked near picnic tables in search of bits of crumbs on the ground. As nervous as the informant was, he didn't seem to notice his beautiful surroundings.

"I also have instructions about getting my family to safety." Ludvik withdrew a manilla envelope.

Drex glanced down at the data transfer between phones. Seventy-five percent complete. "I don't handle that part."

"Please." He pushed the envelope toward him.

Drex's role was information transfer. If this informant was brokering a deal for immunity for himself or his family, then the CIA needed that information—not him. He wondered if the informant would hold back on the rest of the information if his terms weren't met.

"My job—" Drex started to say gently, but a shot rang out, and the informant's head snapped back.

Sniper.

Instinct kicked in, and Drex dove over the back of the bench. He sprinted for cover as pedestrians in the park screamed. His heart thudded, waiting for the second shot intended for him. It didn't come. Whether that was due to obstructing trees or an unwillingness to accidentally hit a civilian, he didn't know.

The shot had probably originated from the Hanavský Pavilion, since the iconic structure gave a panoramic view of the park from the peak. Drex didn't have time to investigate.

Even as he ran and his mind calculated an escape route, he wondered who the shooter could be. Was it someone from the informant's government, the US government, or a third party? And who had discovered their clandestine meeting? The only people who'd known were the two of them and the agency where Drex worked.

Two blocks from the shooting, he caught up with a crowd of tourists walking outside Kouzlo Museum. He slowed to join them—blending in for a few minutes and controlling his breathing so as not to draw attention to himself. He scanned his surroundings for anyone after him as he tugged a baseball cap out of his pocket and pulled it on.

Two men were on the hunt, necks snapping different directions as they searched. Humpty and Dumpty wore black cargo pants, black leather jackets, and intense, scowling expressions. Drex didn't know them or who they worked for, but they were certainly trouble.

When the crowd moved to enter the museum, Drex cut across Valdstejnska Road and through a forecourt on the way to the metro station.

As he continued underground, he pulled out his phone and speed dialed a number. "Chester. Code Brown," he said.

"Oh, no! You about to be rolled up? Are you okay?" the woman asked.

Code Brown was their alert that they'd been played—literally when crap hit the fan. Some type of double-cross was happening, and they needed to cut and run. *Rolled up* was spy code for discovered and captured. Hopefully he wouldn't be, but he'd never been so close to being ensnared before today. He felt like death itself was breathing down his neck.

"I'm working my exit strategy. I'm okay, but this is serious."

"Zielinski?" Chester asked.

Sandra Chester, a feisty black woman in her sixties, had been Drex's assistant since he'd joined Zielinski's team. All of the team worked remotely, so he'd only seen her the few times Zielinski had wanted video conference calls, but they talked several times a week amidst the planning and execution of missions.

"Could be." Drex worked to slow his breathing as he rummaged through tickets—he'd pre-purchased one for the bus, one for the tram, and one for the subway. "Only the three of us knew where the drop would be."

He preferred to cultivate prospective informants himself and build the relationship before acquiring whatever secrets they had, but Drex had stepped into this delivery cold, never having met Ludvik before today. High-risk information exchanges like this were better done *not* in person, but apparently this defector wouldn't hear of it. Based on the bullet through his head, he hadn't made a wise decision.

"You've got your arrangements?" Drex asked his handler after scanning his card and entering the boarding platform.

Despite never meeting face-to-face, he'd bonded with her over the last seven years. Forming attachments in his line of work created an occupational hazard, but he trusted Chester with his life. She'd helped him out of many tough spots and had an uncanny ability to forewarn of danger.

"California will be lovely this time of year," she said.

She wasn't moving to California, and he would never know her exact relocation spot. He hoped it would be somewhere tropical. Jamaica perhaps. She deserved it.

"You have any guidance for me?" he asked.

"The spirits are telling me you should pick B."

He'd never known what to make of Chester's claim to interact with spirits, but he thought of her gift as intuition rather than something other-worldly. And he wholeheartedly trusted Chester's intuition; it had saved him from more than one tight spot.

Option B.

He had five different identities ready for five different cities as contingency plans should something run afoul. While Chester had helped him set up the identities, she didn't know which letter corresponded to which location. In this way, she could never be forced to surrender information about his new life.

Hopefully, she would arrive safely at the tropical paradise destination he envisioned for her and never have to contend with the fallout from this debacle.

"Thank you for everything." He needed to wrap up the

conversation before he lost his cell signal as he stepped onto the train.

"Easy now," Chester said in a sweet, soothing tone. "This doesn't mean goodbye forever. Just for a bit."

"Oh, yeah? Your demons tell you that?" he teased.

She gave him a cluck of disapproval. "Spirits. Not demons."

"Stay safe." He looked down at the envelope in his hand from the defector. Ludvik's dying request.

"You enjoy your next adventure." She disconnected the call.

Next adventure? All he planned to do was lay low and keep his head down. He had no way of knowing if the sniper was from his team, the Czech government, or the CIA. All of these groups would now be after him—either because they wanted the information he now had or because they thought Drex was the traitor.

Holly pulled her office door shut and locked it. She adjusted the hanging green and red wreath. Delightfully warm with Christmas spirit, she barely noticed the biting cold wind. After adjusting her hat and scarf, she practically skipped down the sidewalk.

Tonight was the night. Tonight, Figgy would appear, and for the next twelve days, the two of them would spread Christmas cheer.

She walked the few blocks home, grateful the sidewalk had been cleared. Her exterior Christmas lights blinked white, green, and red. She'd decorated her front door to look like a slender, gift-wrapped present. Too bad the inside of her house wasn't as picturesque as the outside—or at least the outside night view, since daylight revealed peeling paint and tattered shingles.

After unlocking the door, she let herself inside and dropped her keys and purse in the foyer. To the left, her Christmas tree twinkled in the unfinished living room. To her right, the kitchen smelled of paint sealant. At least she had heat.

She'd purchased the older home as a foreclosure. The foundation was in good condition, but everything else was outdated—from the dark wood paneling in the living room to the bland kitchen cabinets to the faded wallpaper in the bathrooms.

Nothing a little TLC couldn't fix—except that the projects seemed never-ending. When she wasn't busy buying and selling homes for her clients, she poured blood, sweat, and tears into her own. Yes, all three of those ingredients from her body had gone into this house.

She hung up her coat in the closet and walked toward the living room fireplace. Could she get the flue working in time to enjoy a fire this Christmas?

Lifting the peppermint scented candle from the mantle, she inhaled the fragrance. She would forever be instantly filled with happiness and fond memories at the smell of peppermint. After setting it back down, she used the lighter beside it to set the wick to flame.

December 12th.

She would let the candle burn tonight—and tomorrow, Figgy McJingles would arrive.

<<<<<<<Keep Reading Holly's Holiday>>>>>>>>>>

Also by CB SAMET:

Magical Romance Novellas

IN BOXED SETS

Individual Books

Sadie's Sprit / Willow's Windfall

Cassie's Chase / Phoebe's Pharaoh

Vanessa's Valentine / Autumn's Angel

Carol's Christmas / Allison's Alibi

Gracelynn's Genie / Michelle's Miracle

Heather's Hero / Chloe's Cupid

Sabrina's Storm / Jenny's Justice

Stella's Star / Gigi's Gift

Phoenix Phantom / Fiona's Freedom

<<<<<<<<<<<<<<********>>>>>>>>>>>>

Romantic Suspense Novels

The Rider File Series:

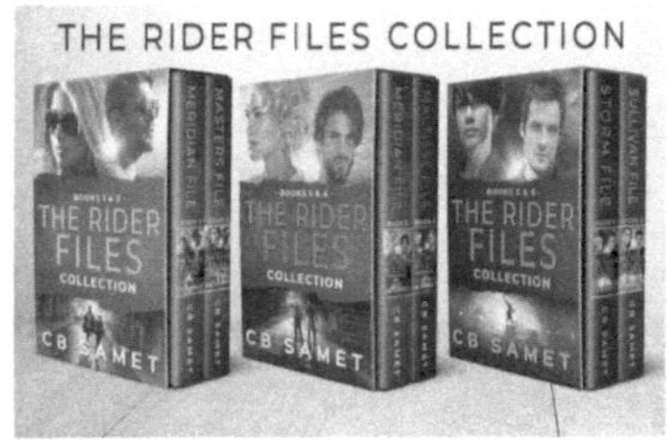

Meridian File / Masters File / Box Set 1

McMillan File / Maltisse File / Box Set 2

Storm File / Sullivan File / Box Set 3

Sharp File / Sizani File / Box Set 4

Rivera File / Rucker File / Box Set 5

2025: Richmond File / Redwood File / Box Set 6

www.ingramcontent.com/pod-product-compliance
Lightning Source LLC
Chambersburg PA
CBHW032042180726
48284CB00008B/2707